Warner Bros.

QUEST FOR CAMELOT

A novelization by J.J. Gardner

Screenplay by Kirk De Micco and William Schifrin

Screen Story by Jacqueline Feather and David Seidler

Based on the novel "The King's Damosel" by Vera Chapman

SCHOLASTIC INC.

New York   Toronto   London   Auckland   Sydney

ISBN 0-590-12058-1

Copyright © 1998 by Warner Bros. QUEST FOR CAMELOT, characters, names, and all related indicia are trademarks of Warner Bros. All rights reserved. Published by Scholastic Inc.

12 11 10 9 8 7 6 5 4 3 2 1   8 9/9 0 1 2 3/0

Printed in the U.S.A.

First Scholastic printing, May 1998

1

Farewell, Father

The whitecapped waves splashed against the shore of the beach. Kayley could feel the spray from the cold seawater against her face. But this did not stop her from riding faster. She gave her pony a gentle nudge with the heels of her feet. Soon she was riding fast enough to catch up with her parents.

Kayley's parents, Sir Lionel and Lady Juliana, had already dismounted from their horses. Lady Juliana's horse was a brown-haired beauty that had trotted elegantly from the castle and across the English countryside. Sir Lionel's horse was a large white-haired steed with a powerful chest and proud snout.

As Kayley reached her parents she leaped off her pony and into her father's waiting arms. Together they rolled down the sandy shore, laughing as they went.

But soon the laughter faded. Kayley felt her heart sink. Suddenly she remembered the reason why she and her parents were spending the morning riding together.

"Father, do you really have to go?" she asked Sir Lionel.

"I'm afraid I must," Sir Lionel replied. "You know the knights will be here soon."

"Father," begged Kayley. "Tell me again why you became a knight."

Kayley's parents smiled knowingly at each other.

"Kayley, you've heard that story a thousand times," said Lady Juliana, hoping to spare her husband the need to repeat it.

"Oh, but it's fine, dear," said Sir Lionel. He picked up a piece of driftwood and drew three large circles in the sand.

"Before you were born," Sir Lionel told Kayley, "the land was dark and treacherous. People were divided. They fought hand to hand."

Kayley became entranced as her father told her the story. She could almost see the images of men fighting inside the three circles in the sand.

"The only hope for peace was in the legend of the sword Excalibur," continued Sir Lionel. "For it was said that only the true king could pull this magical sword from its stone and unite the people. Many tried, but all had failed."

At that point in the story, as she had done many times before, Kayley imagined she saw the great sword Excalibur. It was sticking out of a large stone and surrounded by a glorious aura of light.

"Then on the very day you were born," continued her father, "an unexpected hero stepped forth. His name was Arthur. He was the only one able to pull the sword from the stone. As soon as he did it, everyone knew that he was the true king. With Excalibur by his side, he led us out of darkness. Together we built the greatest kingdom on Earth."

"Camelot!" Kayley shouted proudly.

"Yes," said her father. "As a knight I took an oath to protect King Arthur, Camelot, and Excalibur."

Just then the sound of hoofbeats could be heard. It sounded like an army was approaching.

Kayley jumped up. She looked down the shoreline. "The knights are here!" she cried out with excitement. But soon her excitement withered. For now that the knights had arrived she knew it was time for her father to go away.

Sir Lionel got up and welcomed the knights. There was Sir Edward, Sir William, Sir Richard, Sir Thomas, Sir George, Sir John, and Sir James. Kayley knew them all and greeted them with warm hugs and kisses.

Sir Lionel escorted the knights back to his estate. There they had a great feast. As they ate, the knights spoke of Camelot, King Arthur, and great adventures. Kayley listened to every word, picturing each exciting scene in her mind.

When everyone was done eating, the knights climbed back on their horses. Sir Lionel lifted Kayley up and gave her a kiss good-bye. Then he climbed on his steed and took his place among the other knights.

"United we stand," the knights said in unison. *"Now and forever."*

As soon as they started off, Kayley leaped on her pony and rode after them.

"I'm coming with you, Daddy!" she exclaimed.

"When you're old enough you'll come to

Camelot," replied Sir Lionel. "And then you will do great things. I love you, Kayley."

He waved to her, then picked up speed and rode off beyond her view. Kayley tried to ride after her father, but her pony was not fast enough. Soon she slowed down and returned to her mother.

"One day I will be a knight," said Kayley as she climbed off her horse. "I will be a knight just like Father."

2

The Knights of the Round Table

Sir Lionel and the knights stopped only to eat and sleep as they made their way through the English countryside. The people waved as the famous knights went by. Many brought food and water and offered it to the knights.

"United we stand, now and forever," chanted the knights as they passed through the villages that led to Camelot.

The villagers cheered each time they heard the chant.

Finally, on the fourth day of their journey, Sir Lionel saw a shining fortress on the horizon. The fortress was completely surrounded by a moat of flowing water that shimmered in the sunlight. The walls of the fortress were high and its stones had a golden glow about them. In the sky above the fortress was a rainbow that seemed to stretch out across the countryside itself.

It was Camelot!

The thick drawbridge of Camelot was lowered as soon as Sir Lionel and the knights approached. As they entered the great walled city, all who lived there cheered their return.

The knights' hearts were warmed by the greeting of the people of Camelot. They paraded proudly through the courtyard until they reached a large castle. The castle was the largest building in the whole city. There, standing on the balcony, was a young man. Sir Lionel recognized the man instantly. It was none other than King Arthur.

"It's been ten years, ten wonderful years. Today we gather back at Camelot to celebrate all that made our kingdom great," King Arthur announced upon the knights' arrival. "Liberty and justice for all! Today we shall divide our countryside in equal shares, promising equality for all who live here!"

Everyone, including the knights, cheered King Arthur's promise.

"United we stand! Now and forever!" the knights shouted in unison. *"Hand upon hand, brother to brother! No one shall be greater than all!"* They dismounted from their horses and entered King Arthur's castle.

Inside the castle was a room with an enormous round table. One by one the knights placed their shields in front of them as they took their places around the table.

"Valor!" exclaimed Sir Lionel.

"Justice!" exclaimed Sir Richard.

"Trust!" exclaimed Sir Lancelot.

"Freedom!" exclaimed Sir George.

"Peace!" exclaimed Sir Thomas.

"Honor!" exclaimed Sir William.

"Goodness!" exclaimed Sir Edward.

"Strength!" exclaimed Sir John.

"Valor!" exclaimed Sir James.

King Arthur was smiling. He was proud of his Knights of the Round Table. "Hand upon hand, brother to brother," he said, repeating the knights' chant. "No one shall be greater than —"

"*Me!*" interrupted a voice.

Everyone turned around to see a big, mean-looking knight who was also very fat. It was Sir Ruber. And he was late.

"Sir Ruber!" said King Arthur, glaring at the knight.

"Charming chant," said Sir Ruber. "Now let's get down to business. I've waited a long time for this day. What about my new land?"

"Sir Ruber, always thinking of yourself,"

replied Arthur. "As Knights of the Round Table, our obligation is to the people and not to ourselves. The lands will be divided according to each person's needs."

"Then I need more than everyone," said Sir Ruber. He jumped to his feet and slammed his fists on the table. "I wouldn't have supported you all these years if I thought you were running a charity!"

There was a murmur among the knights. They were shocked by Sir Ruber's behavior.

"The king has decided," Sir Lionel told Sir Ruber, throwing him a fierce look.

"Then it's time for a new king," snarled Sir Ruber. "And I vote for me!" Thereupon, he pulled out a mace from under his uniform and smashed it down on the center of the table. Splinters of wood flew everywhere.

Sir Lionel jumped up. "I will not serve a false king," he told Sir Ruber defiantly.

Sir Ruber growled. "Then serve a dead one," he replied. He pulled his mace from the table and charged after King Arthur.

All at once the knights reached for their swords. They descended upon Ruber and tried to restrain him. But Ruber was too strong. One by one he threw the knights to the ground. Then, his nostrils flaring with rage, he thundered toward Arthur again.

This time King Arthur was ready for traitorous Sir Ruber. In his hand shimmered his sword, the legendary Excalibur.

Sir Ruber was not frightened by the sword. He charged toward King Arthur with his mace.

But King Arthur was too fast for Sir Ruber. He raised Excalibur, blocking Sir Ruber's mace. No sooner had the mace touched Excalibur than — *ZAP!* — the mace exploded into thin air. The shock of the explosion sent Sir Ruber flying across the room and against the far wall.

Ruber groaned with pain as he rose to his feet. "Be warned," he told Arthur and the knights with a clenched fist. "One day that sword will be in my hand. And all of Camelot will be mine!"

This so angered the knights that they charged Sir Ruber, many sending their arrows and spears flying. But Ruber was too quick for them. By the time they reached the door Sir Ruber had fled the castle.

Suddenly, the knights heard King Arthur cry out in horror. "Sir Lionel!" he exclaimed.

The knights quickly spun around. All at once they let out a horrified gasp. For there, on the floor of the Round Table room, lay Sir Lionel. Somehow, in all the turmoil, he had been slain.

3

An Unwelcome Visitor

Word of Sir Lionel's death spread across the land, bringing sadness to everyone. The saddest of all was Sir Lionel's family. His daughter, Kayley, could hardly believe she would never see him again. King Arthur gave Kayley and her mother Sir Lionel's shield and said they would always be welcome at Camelot. Day after day, Kayley stared into the shield at her reflection, still dreaming of becoming a knight.

Many years passed. King Arthur kept his promise and brought freedom and equality to all in the land. Juliana continued to run the family's estate. And Kayley, who had grown up to be a beautiful young woman, helped her mother with all the chores.

Kayley would often think of her father as she did her chores. She remembered what a great knight he was and all the great things he did to help King Arthur. She wondered when she would become a knight herself. But soon she learned that there were no women knights. Still, she longed for the day when she could walk in her father's footsteps and do great things.

Then, one day, word spread across the land that something terrible had happened to the king. A Griffin, with huge wings and sharp claws, had descended upon Camelot. None of the Knights of the Round Table were able to stop the creature. It snatched

Excalibur up in its beak, injuring the king as it did so. Then it rose up into the sky and escaped into the mountains.

King Arthur ordered the knights to find the sword. But try as they did, they could not find the powerful Excalibur. When the knights returned to Camelot empty-handed and forlorn, the king's magician Merlin chanted, "Silver wings, protect the sword."

As soon as Kayley heard of the terrible incident she decided that she must do something to help King Arthur. One day, while trying on a new dress her mother was making for her, she announced that she was going to look for Excalibur herself.

"No! Absolutely not!" replied Juliana.

"But, Mother, Excalibur is missing," insisted Kayley. "I must go after it."

"That's a job for knights, not for a young girl," explained Juliana.

"But I want to be a knight," said Kayley. "I want to go on grand adventures, fighting evil, rescuing damsels in distress! By the way, what is a damsel, anyway?"

Juliana grinned. "Now, Kayley, stand still and let me measure you," she said, changing the subject.

"Mother, I don't want a new dress. I want to save Camelot. If you'd just let me, I know I could find Excalibur on my own."

"The knights will find the sword," replied Juliana. "And they'll do it by working together."

"While I'm working here," said Kayley unhappily. "Doing the chores! Fetching the eggs! Taking care of the house! *Boring!* Where's the glory in that?"

"Kayley, one day you'll learn what Camelot means," said Juliana assuringly. Then she took up the hem of her daughter's new dress. "Until then, you'll stay here with me."

Kayley sighed with disappointment. "Oh, all right," she agreed unhappily.

When her mother was done, Kayley ran

angrily out of the room, across the court-yard, and into the henhouse. There she sat for a long, unhappy while.

"How am I ever going to do great things if I'm stuck here?" she finally asked out loud.

Her thoughts were interrupted. All of a sudden the door to the henhouse flew open. Two big, ugly men scooped up Kayley and carried her back to the castle.

Along the way Kayley saw that her father's land was now full of big, ugly men on horseback, most of whom looked and smelled as if they hadn't taken a bath in months.

Something was terribly wrong. Before she knew it her two kidnappers hid her behind a tapestry in the main hall of the castle.

From behind the tapestry Kayley could see her mother, who seemed very fright-ened. Standing in front of her was a big, menacing fellow wearing a knight's hel-met.

"Who — who are you?" Kayley's mother asked the man.

The man removed his helmet. All at once Kayley could see that her mother now recognized the man.

"Sir Ruber!" said Kayley's mother.

"Juliana," said Sir Ruber with a bow. "I was in the neighborhood and decided to invade."

Now Kayley's mother became enraged. "I demand that you leave immediately!" she ordered Ruber.

"So rude," snapped Ruber. "And after I came all this way just to see you."

"What do you want?" asked Juliana.

Ruber smiled. "Camelot," he replied slyly. "I'm so bored with peace. I want to go back to war and violence. You see, that's my idea of fun."

Ruber picked up Sir Lionel's shield and tossed it at Juliana.

"You're mad!"

"I'm so glad you noticed," said Ruber. "I've been working at it for years. You see, I intend to make King Arthur and his court mine. And, pretty Juliana, you're going to help me."

"I would sooner die," said Juliana in defiance.

"I think you'll find that you won't be able to resist," Ruber said with a laugh. He pulled the tapestry away from the wall and revealed Kayley being held by his two henchmen.

"Mother!" cried Kayley.

Juliana ran to Kayley. "Don't you dare harm her!" she shouted to Ruber.

"Follow my plans and she won't be hurt."

Kayley knew at once that her mother had no choice. She would have to help Sir Ruber conquer Camelot.

4

A Narrow Escape

"Years from now," announced Sir Ruber as he led Juliana and Kayley out into the courtyard, "no one will bother to recall your good King Arthur because all of this land will be mine, mine, *MINE!*"

As he spoke, Ruber lined up his soldiers in a row and made sure that each one had a weapon that was stolen from Sir Lionel's arsenal. Then he explained his plan to Kayley and Juliana.

"You, Juliana, will lead me to Camelot, where I will claim all that is mine," he told her. "My men will hide in the back of your wagons and you'll sit up front. The knights of Camelot trust you and they'll open the gates wide. But first, I'll need to create my mechanical army."

Kayley and her mother watched with horror as Ruber snapped his fingers. One of his henchmen handed Ruber a small vial filled with a bubbling potion. Ruber looked around and grabbed a rooster by the neck.

"With a drop of this potion I bought from some witches," explained Sir Ruber, "this rooster will turn into a weapon that I can use at will."

Ruber pulled an ax out from under his cloak. He threw the rooster, the ax, and a few drops of the magic potion into the courtyard well. An explosion was heard from deep inside the well and smoke rose up from the bottom.

"Behold Bladebeak!" exclaimed Ruber, pointing at the well.

Thereupon a horrifying creature rose up out of the well. What was once the rooster had now become a terrifying giant bird with a sharp, glistening ax for a beak.

Kayley cringed at the sight of the creature.

One by one, Sir Ruber threw his soldiers into the well. Each soldier was followed by a weapon. Like the rooster, when each man returned from the well he had changed into a monster. One now had two deadly maces where his arms used to be. Another had hands that had been changed into a bow and arrow. Yet another returned with swords for his arms.

Suddenly Kayley felt her mother tug at her shoulders. "Go to Camelot," her mother whispered. Then she pointed to an opening in the courtyard wall that was just big enough for Kayley to escape through. "Warn King Arthur," she said.

"I won't leave you here," said Kayley.

But her mother insisted. "Kayley, Ruber will be in Camelot in three days. Take the main road. Get there before us."

"But, Mother —"

"Go," said Juliana. "You're our only hope. And be careful, dear."

Kayley realized that her mother was right. While everyone's attention was on Ruber and his new indestructible minions, she could wriggle through the opening in the wall and run off.

Just then a loud, monstrous roar was heard from above. Everyone looked up. It was the Griffin, swooping down into the courtyard, its huge flapping wings creating a sudden gust of wind.

"Ah, my faithful pet," said Sir Ruber as he greeted the Griffin. "How was the flight? Panic sweeps across the land."

"Precisely, master," replied the Griffin.

"And now Excalibur is mine," said Ruber. He gleefully held out his hands as if waiting for the Griffin to give him some great treasure. Kayley realized that it was Sir Ruber who had sent the Griffin to steal Excalibur.

"Here's where we enter a gray area," said the Griffin, nervously clearing its throat.

Sir Ruber became very angry. "Excuse me," he said. "You *lost* Excalibur? How?"

"I was attacked . . . by a falcon," replied the Griffin.

"What? My magnificent beast outmatched by a puny little pigeon?"

"It wasn't a pigeon," insisted the Griffin. "It was a falcon with silver wings."

"Silver wings? Oooh, scary," said Ruber, making fun of the Griffin. "Where is the sword now?"

"In a place of untold danger . . ." the Griffin started to answer. "I dropped it in the Forbidden Forest."

"The Forbidden Forest?!" exclaimed Sir Ruber. There was a murmur of fear among Sir Ruber's minions. Everyone was afraid of the Forbidden Forest.

"Precisely, master," said the Griffin.

"Have I told you today how magnificently and totally stupid you are?" Ruber asked the Griffin. "Excalibur is the one thing that can keep me from my conquest of Camelot!"

Suddenly the pounding of hoofbeats was heard. Everyone turned toward the sound. Someone was escaping on horseback. It was Kayley!

"The girl!" exclaimed Ruber. Then he pointed to his minions. "You! Bladebeak! Spike Slinger! Bowhands! After her! Bring her back!"

The creatures gave chase after Kayley just as swiftly as they could.

"And you," Ruber said, grabbing the Griffin by the neck. "You are going to lead me to *Excalibur!*"

5

The Man in the Forest

Kayley steered her pony away from her home. She rode as fast as she could. She knew that at top speed she would reach Camelot in a few days. Then she could warn King Arthur about Sir Ruber.

But no sooner had she picked up speed than she heard something behind her. She turned around. Ruber's horrible creatures were chasing her. And they were catching up!

Kayley was frightened but continued bravely on. After a few minutes she came upon a fork in the road and a sign that read:

MAIN ROAD TO CAMELOT
AND FORBIDDEN FOREST

Kayley thought for a moment. She wanted to escape from Ruber's creatures, but she didn't want to lead them to Camelot. So, taking a deep, courageous breath, she took the road that led to the Forbidden Forest.

Ruber's minions followed her, just as she had hoped. After a short time she saw the dark, foreboding forest up ahead. Kayley's pony, frightened at the sight, whinnied and reared with fear. Kayley went flying to the ground.

Kayley rose to her feet, uninjured.

She looked back at the approaching minions.

"The Forbidden Forest," Kayley said to herself, realizing that the frightening woods were her only chance of escape. So with all the courage she could drum up she ran into the forest.

Once inside, a chill went through Kayley's body. The forest was dark and dense and scary. She had to cover her face to shield herself from the sharp branches that jutted out from the trees.

She came upon a narrow crevice in a rock and started to squeeze through. Suddenly a huge mace came down and shattered the rock to bits. Kayley looked up and cringed with terror. It was Spike Slinger who had smashed the rock. And with him were Bowhands and Bladebeak. The horrible minions had followed her into the forest!

Kayley thought for certain that all was lost. She ran for her life, but the minions followed close behind.

All this noisy activity seemed to have a strange effect on the Forbidden Forest. As if awakened from a sleep, the plants and mud of the forest suddenly came to life. The plants began to wriggle and squirm like snakes. Podlike monsters began to form out of the muddy ground. One of the plants grabbed hold of Kayley.

Kayley narrowly escaped its clutches but she tripped, tumbled down a hill, and fell into a stream. Shaken, Kayley tried to stand up — only to find she'd gotten tangled up in a huge fishing net.

"Hey! That's my net!" shouted someone from behind a tree. And with that, a young man jumped out.

At that very moment Bladebeak and Bowhands appeared. Upon seeing the man, Spike Slinger grabbed Bladebeak. Then he hurled the monstrous rooster straight at the young man. Kayley thought for sure he was doomed. But just then, she heard a chirping sound — and the young man moved out of the way of Bladebeak's hatchet just in time.

Next, Spike Slinger and Bowhands

rushed the young man. But by the time they moved to attack him, the man side-stepped their blows. Kayley watched, fascinated by the man's battle skills. Then she noticed a beautiful falcon with glistening silver feathers flying near the man. Each time one of Ruber's minions would attack, the falcon would chirp. Kayley realized that the silver falcon was helping the man by telling him where the minions were. But why was the bird doing this, Kayley wondered? Couldn't the man see the minions for himself?

But even the falcon couldn't catch every move of the minions. Spike Slinger cornered the man and pinned him to a tree. Instantly, the man reached up and pulled at a vine. This sent some logs from above tumbling down on Spike Slinger, who tumbled into a plant monster. The monster opened up its mouth and swallowed Spike Slinger whole!

Next, Bowhands charged the young man again. This time the falcon was able to

31

warn the man. The man swerved around and set off a booby trap, throwing Bowhands onto a mound of land. Suddenly the land turned into a big, wet, hungry mouth. It opened up wide and wrapped its tongue of seaweed around Bowhands. Then it sucked Bowhands inside like a tasty dessert!

"That was *incredible*!" exclaimed Kayley as the young man approached her. "How you smashed those creatures," she continued. "How you avoided that thing. You're amazing! You're — you're — you're not even listening to me!"

Kayley was right. The young man was busy pulling his fishing net out of the swampy water. It was torn to shreds.

"Great." He sighed. "It took me six weeks to make this net."

"Your net?" asked Kayley. "But you saved my life. Thank you."

"Well, anyone can make a mistake," grumbled the young man.

"Oh, I get it," said Kayley, insulted. "This is where King Arthur sends in his unfunny jesters, right?"

The young man turned and approached Kayley.

"And now I'll thank you," said the man.

"For what?" Kayley asked, confused.

"For reminding me why I'm a hermit," said the man. "Good day." And with that he turned and walked away.

"Wait!" called Kayley. She ran after the young man. "What's your name?"

"It's Garrett," replied the man as he continued away.

"I'm Kayley. Hey, why don't you look at me when I'm talking to you?"

Just then Kayley caught a glimpse of Garrett's eyes. They seemed to look right past her, as if they couldn't see. Then Kayley realized that Garrett really couldn't see at all.

"Oh," she said. "I didn't realize that you were —"

"Tall? Rugged? Handsome?" asked Garrett.

"Blind."

"You know, I always forget that one," said Garrett. Then he walked away. As he did so, the silver falcon that had helped him earlier followed behind. All at once it spread its silver wings and began chirping loudly, as if it were trying to tell Garrett something.

"Not now, Ayden," Garrett said to the falcon.

"Hey, your falcon has silver wings," said Kayley.

"Really?" replied Garrett. "I'll have to take your word for it."

"It means he knows where Excalibur is," explained Kayley.

"Sure he does," said Garrett. "In Camelot. You know: big castle, lots of flags."

"No, it's somewhere in the forest. Ruber has stolen it and he has taken my mother hostage. That's why I'm here. I must find the sword and return it to Arthur, or Camelot and my mother are doomed."

Now Ayden the silver falcon began chirping more insistently. This finally made Garrett stop and take notice.

"You mean Excalibur *is* here?" Garrett asked the bird. "Right! Then we're going after it!"

"Great!" exclaimed Kayley happily.

"Not you," said Garrett. "Me and Ayden. We work alone."

But Kayley was not to be stopped from finding Excalibur. "Well," she said, "I see no reason why I can't come along."

6

Two Heads Are
Not Always Better
Than One

"I know each rock and stone in this forgotten place," Garrett told Kayley as they walked through the mysterious forest. He spoke plainly and firmly as if he were trying to make something perfectly clear. "In here I embrace what others fear. In fact, this is my world and I share it with no one.

I've seen your world. I've felt its pain. I've heard all its lies. But in this forest I stand alone."

"I stand alone, too," said Kayley when Garrett had finished. "I just need your help this once."

Ayden flew to Kayley and landed on her shoulder. The silver falcon chirped loudly in agreement.

"I can see there's no winning with you two," admitted Garrett. "All right, all right, I'll help you. But don't give me any trouble!"

Just then a concerned look came over Garrett's face. He stopped and sniffed the air.

"Have you got a cold?" asked Kayley.

"Shhh!" ordered Garrett. Then he sniffed the air again.

"What is it?" asked Kayley insistently.

"We're in dragon country," replied Garrett.

"Oooh, right," said Kayley, joking. She didn't believe in dragons. "Are you sure this is dragon country? I mean, it's not like there's a sign or anything saying 'Welcome to Dragon Country.'"

As they continued on, the forest became even more eerie. The land had become more ashen and rocky. And all the trees nearby were dead.

"Do you think we'll see any dragons?" Kayley asked nervously as they walked on. "By the way, is a group of dragons a pack or a flock? A gaggle or a pride? Is it a herd or a —"

"Quiet!" insisted Garrett.

"Do you hear something?"

"No," replied Garrett. "I just want you to be *quiet*."

All of a sudden a big shadow fell over Kayley and Garrett. They froze in their tracks. Something had snuck up behind them. Something *big*. It was a huge, ferocious-looking dragon!

At once Kayley and Garrett ran for cover inside a nearby nest of hatched dragon shells. The shells were just big enough for them to hide in. For a moment they felt safe. But soon they sensed another presence nearby.

"Dragons!" exclaimed Kayley, frightened.

"Where?" came an unfamiliar voice, sounding just as frightened as Kayley. *"I don't see any dragons."*

Both Kayley and Garrett peeked out from the eggshells to find out who the strange new voice belonged to. Much to their surprise, it belonged to a dragon that was hiding in another eggshell. It was a very strange dragon because it had not one head, but *two*. And both heads were shaking with fear.

"What do you mean you don't see any dragons?" Kayley asked the two-headed creature. "You're dragons!"

"Oh, heavens," said one of the dragon's heads upon seeing Kayley and Garrett. "Someone's found our hiding place."

Then the two-headed dragon hid back behind the eggshell.

"Shut up, Cricket-ball," said one of the dragon's heads. "Let me handle this." First he made a puppet shadow of a ferocious dragon. The shadow loomed against a nearby wall. Then he began to roar and roar just as frightfully as he could. "We are dragons! Ferocious, hungry dragons!"

Kayley's eyes widened with fear.

"Good show, Corny," said the first dragon head. "That is clever. Let me have a go." And with that he also made a puppet shadow and began to roar. But instead of a shadow of a ferocious dragon, his looked like a meek bunny rabbit.

Suddenly Kayley wasn't frightened at all.

"Oh, great," said the second head. "The bunny rabbit of death. They're probably cringing with fear." And with that the second dragon head began walloping the first. Then the first one punched back. In no time at all the dragon heads were beating each other up.

At this point Garrett had had enough. He raised his staff and brought it down on the dragon's eggshell, splitting it in two. The dragon tumbled out of the shell.

"Please don't hurt us," said one of the heads, cowering with fear at Garrett's staff.

At that Garrett tapped the two heads of the dragon with the staff.

"Hey!" said the other dragon head. "Easy with the stick, buddy!"

"What *are* you?" asked Garrett, quizzically.

"What do you think we are?" said the first dragon head. "We're a two-headed dragon."

"And the ladies have arrived," said the other head upon seeing Kayley, who had gotten out of the eggshell for a closer look. "Hello, sweetheart. Ever met a real dragon?"

The two-headed dragon bowed and curtsied for Kayley.

"Enchanted, *mademoiselle*," said the first dragon head. "My name is Devon. And this growth on my neck is Cornwall."

"But you can call me Corny for short," the other head told Kayley, with a blush.

"Yes," said Devon. "Short on wit, manners, and charm. Everything I hold dear."

"How about holding your breath?" quipped Cornwall.

"I'm surprised you haven't fried each other yet," sighed Garrett.

"Fry?" replied Devon. "We don't even simmer." And with that Devon burped out a pathetic puff of smoke.

"Yeah," admitted Cornwall. "You see, unlike most dragons, *he* can't breathe fire or fly. Sad, really."

"*Excusez-moi*, Mr. Self-denial," said Devon, pointing to their unusually small dragon wings. "But *we* can't breathe fire or fly."

"Only 'cause you're holding me back," retorted Cornwall. "If I didn't have you I could do a lot of things. I'd rock with the dinos! Swing with the rhinos! I'd be the dragon king!"

That made Devon mad. "How about if I didn't have you?" he shot back. "I could be anything I wanted if there was only me!"

"You guys have gotta stop your bickering and get your act together," interjected Kayley.

"Did someone say act?" asked Devon. "I have an act, but it's a *solo* career! I'd be a fire-breathing lizard. Why, if I had separate parts I could be a star at Camelot! I'm trapped! Trapped!"

"Stuck here with you for five hundred years," added Cornwall.

"Oh, you've learned to count," said Devon.

"If you got me a good lawyer I woulda split four hundred years ago," said Cornwall.

"I didn't come here to be insulted," said Devon.

"Oh?" asked Cornwall. "Where do you usually go?"

"You'd be nothing without me," Devon told Cornwall.

"I'm so tired of your naggin'," groaned Cornwall.

"And I'm so tired of your braggin'!" Devon groaned back.

By this time, Kayley and Garrett had had quite enough of the dragon's spat. They started to walk away.

"Hey, where're you going?" Cornwall called after them.

"To save Camelot!" Kayley shouted back.

"Camelot?" asked Devon. "The restaurants! The theaters! The dragons!"

"The dragons?" repeated Cornwall, fearfully.

"Quick, let's hide," said Devon.

"But what about that girl? And that *schmo* with the stick?"

"Not my problem," said Devon, already scoping out a hiding place.

"If we help them, they might take us to Camelot," said Cornwall.

This idea appealed to Devon. "Well, let's save the humans then!" he said.

Devon and Cornwall could not have

made a better decision. For at that very moment a huge, fierce dragon swooped down from the sky and began blowing fire at them.

"This way!" Cornwall shouted to Kayley and Garrett.

Kayley and Garrett followed the two-headed dragon along a road with a rocky path until they reached a lake. But it was like no lake Kayley had ever seen before. This lake had eerie vapors rising out of it.

"Wait," said Kayley upon seeing the lake. "What is this?"

"Don't worry," Devon assured her. "It's perfectly safe."

With the chirping Ayden as his guide, Garrett placed the tip of his staff in the lake. As soon as it touched the vapors it began to sizzle. Garrett could tell at once the lake was filled with deadly acid.

"Safe?" asked Garrett.

"So long as you don't step in it," said Cornwall.

Devon and Cornwall led Kayley and Garrett across the lake by stepping gingerly on a path of stepping-stones. They had to cross as fast as they could, for by now another menacing dragon was swooping down on them.

Once on the other side they looked for a place to hide and saw a cave. But no sooner had they started than Cornwall shrieked and pointed up ahead.

"Look!" he exclaimed. "Another dragon!"

"That's not a dragon," said Kayley, tightening her lips. "It's the Griffin and Sir Ruber. They found us!"

The castle at Camelot was
built around the Ring of Stones.

When Kayley was small,
she loved listening to her father,
Sir Lionel, tell tales of the Knights
of the Round Table and the magic
sword Excalibur.

Sir Lionel told Kayley about the legend. "It was said that
only the true king could pull this magical sword from its
stone and unite the people."

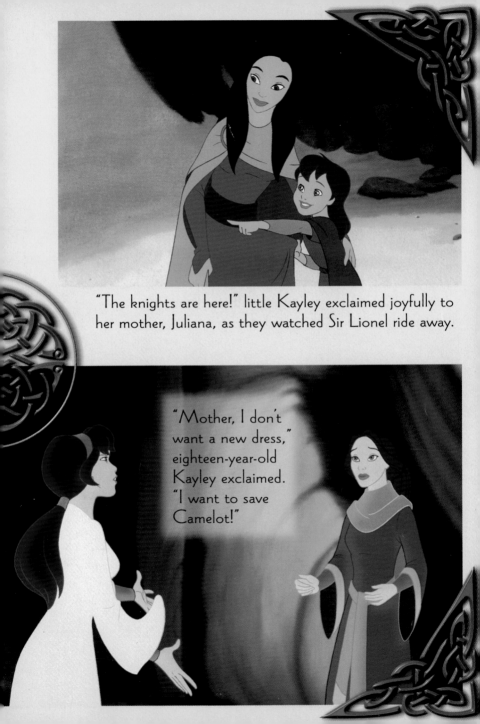

"The knights are here!" little Kayley exclaimed joyfully to her mother, Juliana, as they watched Sir Lionel ride away.

"Mother, I don't want a new dress," eighteen-year-old Kayley exclaimed. "I want to save Camelot!"

"Juliana, I was in the neighborhood and I thought I'd invade," evil Sir Ruber snarled.

When Ruber's back was turned, Kayley escaped on horseback.

"Behold, Bladebeak!" Sir Ruber had turned a rooster into a weapon!

"Excuse me, you lost Excalibur?" Ruber, furious, demanded of the Griffin, a mythical beast with the head of an eagle and the body of a lion.

Scared but determined, Kayley
entered the Forbidden Forest.

"It took me six weeks to build this net," Garrett grumbled
after saving Kayley.

"I'm Devon, and this growth on my neck is Cornwall," quipped the bickering two-headed dragon.

"Garrett, let's take them with us, please," Kayley begged on behalf of Devon and Cornwall.

"Ayden taught me all the secrets of the forest,"
Garrett explained to Kayley.

Kayley, victorious,
returned the magic
sword Excalibur
to King Arthur.

7

Garrett's Story

"Quick! Down here!" shouted Cornwall. And with that he and Devon led Kayley and Garrett into the mouth of the nearby cave.

Inside, the cave was dark and musty and scary.

"Are you sure we're safe in here?" asked Kayley.

"It's a lot safer in here than it is out there," replied Cornwall.

47

"We know all the best escape routes," added Devon.

"We've been dodgin' those dragon bullies since we were two hundred years old," explained Cornwall.

"Were we ever that young?" asked Devon.

Devon and Cornwall began to lead Kayley and Garrett deep into the cave. Although it was dark, the two-headed dragon knew every nook and turn. Before long they emerged from an entrance on the other end of the cave. From there they could see dragon country far in the distance. Sir Ruber and his minions were fighting it out with the dragons.

"Well, the good news is we're out of dragon country," Garrett said to Devon and Cornwall. "The better news is that this is where we say good-bye."

"But you can't leave us here," said Devon. "If we try to go back we'll be banished, ostracized, exiled."

"Not to mention kicked out," added Cornwall.

"Why?" asked Kayley.

"We just broke the dragon's cardinal rule," said Cornwall.

"What? *Never wear brown shoes with a blue suit?*" joked Devon.

"No, you moron," replied Cornwall. *"Never help a human."*

But Garrett just ignored the two bickering dragon heads. "C'mon, Kayley," he said. "We must make camp before dark."

"Oh, we can do camp!" said Devon, trying to be helpful.

"Garrett, let's take them with us," pleaded Kayley. "Please."

Garrett sighed. "I suppose you can come along," he said, sounding as if it were against his better judgment. "But *no more complaining!*"

Devon and Cornwall agreed. Then they followed Garrett and Kayley down the mountainside and deeper into the Forbidden Forest.

For the rest of the day everyone searched for Excalibur. They looked inside caves and birds' nests. They looked under rocks and in swamps.

They had to be careful everywhere they went. They knew that at any minute something in the forest could come to life and attack them. They also knew that Sir Ruber was probably not far behind.

"Here's where we stop," said Garrett as night started to fall.

"Stop?" asked Kayley. "But we must get Excalibur."

"Sorry," said Garrett. "No one travels through the Forbidden Forest after dark."

"My father, Sir Lionel, would have," Kayley said defiantly. She walked away and began to sulk.

In the meantime Devon and Cornwall had begun rubbing two sticks together. They were attempting to start a campfire. Yet no matter how hard they tried, they could not start a spark. They threw down the sticks in frustration. Then, much to their surprise, the sticks got up and walked away, laughing as they did so.

By then Garrett had walked over to Kayley, who was staring into the forest, deep in thought.

"Kayley," he began. "I knew your father."

Kayley was stunned. "You did?" she asked, wide-eyed.

"I used to live in Camelot," said Garrett. "I was a stable boy. But I dreamed of becoming a knight. One day there was a fire in the stable. I rushed to save the horses, but I was hurt. The horses began to stampede. By accident, one of them kicked me in the head. Soon all I could see were shadows and shapes. Finally, my world went black. I could see no more.

"After I lost my sight, your father was the only one who still believed in me. He taught me that a knight's strength comes from his heart and his loyalty to the oath of Camelot. I remember the oath: *'United we stand, now and forever.'* Any hope I had of becoming a knight died with him."

Kayley was overwhelmed with emotion. "I felt that way, too," she told Garrett as tears fell from her eyes. "But I knew he would never want me to give up. He wouldn't want you to give up, either. You're as good as any knight in Camelot."

"You really think so?" asked Garrett. Then he walked away. Kayley knew that Garrett didn't believe her.

Garrett started to make a bed out of sticks and brush. Ayden helped, flying up a tree and returning with small twigs and the like.

"How did you find Ayden?" Kayley asked, petting the silver-winged falcon.

"I didn't," answered Garrett. "He found me. He taught me the secrets of the forest: what can heal you, what can hurt you. With Ayden as my eyes, I can survive anything. Here, I'll show you."

Garrett walked over to a flower that was just as tall as he was. Planting his feet firmly, he looked the flower squarely in its petals.

"I take my position and face my fears," he said. Then he tapped the stem of the flower.

The flower mysteriously opened up. "I hold my ground until the last possible moment and wait for Ayden's signal." Now the flower, which seemed to be very annoyed at the intrusion, lunged at Garrett. But just before the flower reached Garrett, Ayden let out a loud chirp of warning. At that signal, Garrett leaped out of the way of the flower.

"Now you try it," Garrett told Kayley, placing her in front of the flower.

"All right," said Kayley. "No problem."

"Take position," said Garrett.

"Take position," repeated Kayley, planting her feet firmly on the ground.

"Face your fears and hold your ground until the last possible moment." Once again Garrett tapped the stem of the plant. Once again it opened up. Upon seeing the opening plant Kayley panicked and tried to get out of its way. The plant reached out and punched her. Kayley fell back, but her fall was broken by Garrett's waiting arms.

"Well, you moved too soon," said Garrett.

"Uh-huh," said Kayley, happy that Garrett had caught her. Suddenly she realized that she felt safe in Garrett's arms. Slowly, she had come to like Garrett very much. With his arms around her now she even thought she might be falling in love with him.

And she could tell from Garrett's expression that he felt the same way, too.

The next morning everyone was awakened by Ayden, who was frantically chirping at the top of his lungs.

Garrett immediately knew why Ayden was chirping. "Ayden's spotted Excalibur," he said as he and the others rose from their beds of brush and sticks. "It must be near. C'mon."

Garrett, Kayley, Devon, and Cornwall followed Ayden a short way through the forest until they came upon a mountain ledge. Once there, Ayden began to fly in circles and chirp frantically.

"Excalibur's close," said Garrett.

"Look!" exclaimed Kayley, pointing to a vine. Hanging from a thorn on the vine was a torn piece of cloth with the seal of Camelot on it.

"This must be from Camelot!" said Kayley. "But where's the sword?"

"Someone must have taken it," Garrett deduced. "Or some*thing* . . ."

And with that Garrett tapped the ground. Everyone looked down with a shudder. For they weren't standing on a mountain ledge at all. They were standing in a huge footprint!

8

The Healing Leaf

"Now we'll never find Excalibur in time," said Kayley. She could only imagine what horrible forest creature had stolen Excalibur.

"If we follow these tracks we will," said Garrett.

But Kayley wasn't listening. "This is all your fault," she told Garrett.

"My fault?" asked Garrett, with surprise.

"Yes," replied Kayley. "If we hadn't stopped —"

"Quiet!" said Garrett.

"We should have kept going —" insisted Kayley.

"Shhh!" said Garrett.

"But I have to save my mother!"

"Please," insisted Garrett. "I'm trying to hear."

"Hear what?" asked Kayley. But no sooner had she asked than an arrow came from out of nowhere and pierced Garrett in his side. Garrett fell down, groaning with pain.

"Garrett!" shrieked Kayley.

"Seize them!" came a voice from behind. Kayley's heart jumped. It was Sir Ruber. And with him were the Griffin, Bladebeak, and Spike Slinger.

"No!" screamed Kayley as Ruber's minions began to descend on them.

With the last of his strength Garrett managed to smash Ruber in the kneecaps with his staff. Ruber grabbed his knees and howled with pain. That gave Kayley just enough time. She quickly pulled Garrett out of the way before Ruber's minions could pounce on him.

Kayley helped Garrett to his feet, but before they could hobble away Ruber and the monsters were after them again.

Kayley thought quickly. She tied a rope to one of the trees of the Forbidden Forest. By doing this she woke up the tree. Upon seeing the commotion that disturbed it, the tree turned into a terrible troll-like monster.

Without losing a second, Kayley, Devon, and Cornwall dragged the injured Garrett away from the tree troll. Now only Ruber and his monsters were in its view. With a great roar the tree attacked. Soon, Ruber and his minions were so occupied with saving themselves from the tree that Kayley and the others had plenty of time to flee to safety.

No sooner had Kayley and the others fled deeper into the forest than dark storm clouds began to form in the sky. Suddenly there was a loud *boom* of thunder and a bright flash of lightning. The wind became very strong and the rain started to fall. And it was becoming very hard to see.

Ayden swooped down and called for everyone to follow him. He guided them across a stream and led them to some large boulders that had formed in the shape of a cave. Everyone stepped inside the cave where they were able to escape the storm.

But all was still not well. Garrett was in great pain from his wound. He lay on the ground groaning.

Kayley looked helplessly at Ayden. Then she looked at Devon and Cornwall. No one knew what to do for Garrett. Everyone was worried that he might die.

Kayley plucked a leaf off a nearby bush and placed it on Garrett's wound. She knew it to be a leaf with magical healing powers. She hoped this would make him feel better.

"Please don't die," she told Garrett, squeezing his hand. "I can't do this on my own. I'm sorry. It's all my fault you were hurt. I was rattling on when I should have been quiet. I'm no help to anyone."

Kayley turned away.

"No," said Garrett weakly. "You're wrong. You know what I see in your eyes, Kayley?"

Kayley turned around. "My eyes?" she asked, surprised. She knew he couldn't *really* "see." But he could visualize. And his feelings were strong.

"Yes," Garrett said, struggling to speak. "Your eyes remind me of the heavens when they sparkle with sunlight."

"They do?"

"Yes," said Garrett. "I see a night I wish could last forever. A night filled with sunlight."

"Oh, Garrett," said Kayley, teardrops forming in her eyes. Now she wanted more than ever for him to live. "I see the same thing in your eyes."

"You do?" asked Garrett, weakly.

"Yes," said Kayley. "I, too, see the heavens and the stars and the sun in the night."

Garrett and Kayley smiled at each other. Each one admitted silently that they loved the other. Kayley felt drawn to Garrett. She leaned forward to kiss him.

But just before their lips could touch, the leaf Kayley had placed on Garrett's wound began to pulsate and glow. Suddenly Garrett began to squirm. He clutched his side and grimaced with pain.

Then, just as suddenly as it started, the plant stopped glowing. Seconds later it dropped away from Garrett's side.

Garrett remained still.

"Is he — is he — ?" asked Devon and Cornwall with concern.

Kayley turned away and lowered her head. She was fearful she had lost Garrett forever.

"The heavens . . . the stars . . . the sun in the night." A voice suddenly came from behind Kayley. "That's what I see in your eyes."

Kayley spun around. It was Garrett! And he was alive!

"Garrett!" said Kayley rushing into his arms. Garrett eagerly embraced her.

Devon and Cornwall cheered with joy. The healing leaf had worked.

Soon Kayley, Garrett, and the dragon were on their way again. With Ayden as their guide they followed the huge tracks that they hoped would lead them to Excalibur. Eventually the tracks led them to the entrance of a deep, dark cave.

All of a sudden they heard a loud booming sound.

"I hope that was your stomach," Kayley said to Devon and Cornwall, nervously.

"No," said Garrett. "That was just the Ogre!"

"The Ogre!?" Devon and Cornwall said, trembling. They started to twist and turn,

looking for any way out. "Well, see ya', good luck, have a nice life, whatever's left of it —"

Kayley was confused. "What's so scary about an Ogre?" she asked.

Suddenly, as if in answer to her question, a huge dragon skeleton came flying out of the cave. It landed right at Kayley's feet.

"Its appetite," Devon and Cornwall answered upon seeing the bones.

Just then came a frightening roar. The ground began to quake at the pounding of huge, heavy footsteps. A second later, a gigantic, ugly foot with long, curled, pointed toenails came out of the cave and headed right for them!

9

The Ogre's Lair

"Get out of the way!" shouted Garrett. Everyone dived for cover.

No sooner were they a safe distance away than they saw the huge creature, nearly the size of a full-grown tree. It was the ugliest creature they had ever seen.

One by one the Ogre threw more huge dragon bones away. Devon and Cornwall swallowed with fear as they watched each bone hit the ground.

"What's he doing?" Kayley wondered.

"I think he's taking out the garbage," said Garrett as he heard each bone drop.

When he was finished, the Ogre turned and headed back into his cave. As he turned, a scabbard, the kind usually used to hold a knife or a sword, fell from his leg. Kayley recognized the seal on the scabbard at once. It was the seal of Camelot.

"That scabbard belongs to King Arthur!" she exclaimed. "He *does* have Excalibur!"

Thinking quickly, Garrett came up with a plan. He motioned for Kayley and the dragon to follow him into the cave. Once inside they found themselves walking through a maze of bones, skeletons, and garbage. It smelled terrible!

"Ogres sleep in the day," he told everyone. "We'll wait for him to fall asleep and then we'll grab the sword."

"Define 'we,'" Cornwall demanded nervously.

"Is we 'us'?" asked Devon, just as nervous.

"Quiet!" Garrett ordered the dragon. "The slightest noise and we're finished."

They moved forward. As they did the cave became darker and darker.

Soon the darkness gave way to an enormous cavern. Its walls were sprinkled with tunnels, and shafts of light beamed through tiny holes in the ceiling.

"Where's Excalibur?" Garrett whispered to the others. "Is it here?"

"He's using it as a toothpick," answered Kayley.

Indeed, the Ogre was leaning against the far wall of the cavern finishing up what looked like a very tasty meal of tree monster. With one hand he tossed away the remains. With the other he was holding the magical sword Excalibur, carefully using it to pick his pointed teeth clean.

"Tell me when he falls asleep," said Garrett.

Sooner, not later, the Ogre belched. Then he drifted off into what looked like a satisfying, deep sleep.

Once Garrett could hear the Ogre snoring he said, "Describe the layout."

"There's a ledge that hangs just above the sword," said Kayley, describing the cavern as best she could. "But it must be a twenty-foot drop."

Garrett formed an image of the cavern in his mind. Then he took his staff and began measuring Kayley and the dragon as if he were fitting them for new clothes.

"What are you planning to do?" Kayley asked Garrett.

"I'm planning to get Excalibur," replied Garrett.

He told Kayley and the dragon his plan. It was risky, but everyone agreed to give it a try.

First, Garrett held Kayley by her ankles and carefully lowered her over the ledge. She reached out but was too far away to clutch Excalibur. Next, Devon and Cornwall lifted Garrett by his legs and lowered him over the ledge while he held Kayley. The group was now like a long chain.

"Lower me down more," said Kayley, her arms struggling to reach the magical sword. "A bit lower."

Devon and Cornwall lowered Garrett a little further. Now Kayley was almost within reach of the sword.

Just then something crashed through the piles of discarded bones that lay all over the cavern floor. The sound startled everyone, especially Devon and Cornwall, who almost lost their grip on Garrett's legs.

"Oh, no," said Devon. "It's him!"

"Who?" asked Garrett. But he didn't have to wait for an answer. A second later he could smell who it was.

It was Sir Ruber. And he wasn't alone.

10

Narrow Escape

"Boss, look, it's Excalibur!" Kayley heard Spike Slinger say to Sir Ruber.

"I hate Ogres," replied Ruber.

Kayley saw Ruber motion to the Griffin to fly over and grab the magical sword. Now she knew she had to get hold of Excalibur before Ruber did. But the wind from the Griffin's long wings began to kick up a lot of dust.

"AH-AH-*CHOO!*" sneezed the Griffin.

The sneeze was so loud it nearly stirred the Ogre out of his deep sleep. Slowly, the horrid creature opened one of its eyes.

Kayley had to think fast. "Nap time's over," she told Garrett. "Quick! Swing me back and forth!"

Garrett immediately began swinging Kayley just like a pendulum. The Ogre, upon seeing Kayley sway back and forth in front of his eyes, became hypnotized by her. That was exactly what Kayley had wanted.

"You are getting very sleeeeepy . . ." she said to the Ogre in a droning tone of voice. "Verrry sleeepy . . ."

The Ogre became groggy again. He slowly shut his eyes and fell back to sleep.

Quickly, Kayley snatched Excalibur from the Ogre's hand.

"I've got it!" she shouted. Devon and Cornwall quickly pulled her and Garrett up to safety.

"Get them!" they heard Sir Ruber order his minions below.

Upon hearing that, Kayley and her friends looked for a way to escape.

"That way!" shouted Devon.

"No! This way!" shouted Cornwall.

"Through that tunnel hole!" said Kayley, pointing to a way out.

Fortunately for them the Ogre had not quite fallen completely to sleep. It was just then that he let out a big yawn, the biggest yawn they had heard anybody ever make. His yawn caused such a wind that it blew Sir Ruber and the Griffin up to the top of the cave.

When they fell back down they landed right next to the Ogre. It was then the Ogre felt the need for a relaxing stretch. He stretched his arms wide and, in the process, pinned Ruber's monstrous minions to the wall. Then he turned on his side and rolled on top of Ruber and the Griffin.

They were all trapped and unable to move.

Meanwhile, Kayley and the others took the opportunity to escape through one of the cavern's tunnels. But when they came out on the other side of the hole they found themselves standing at the edge of a high cliff.

"There's no way out!" exclaimed Devon.

"There's one way out," Kayley told the dragon. "You'll have to fly."

"Fly?" Cornwall and Devon said together. They were terrified of the idea. "That's going to be a problem."

"Why?" asked Kayley.

"Because," they replied. "Neither one of us has ever flown before!"

11

At the End of the Forbidden Forest

Devon and Cornwall realized there was little time for hesitation. They were certain that if they waited any longer Sir Ruber and his army would soon be upon them. Then all would be lost.

If flying was the only way to bring Excalibur back to Camelot, then flying it was going to have to be.

So, with Kayley and Garrett holding on, the dragon took a deep breath and leaped off the high cliff.

They flapped and flapped their wings, but instead of going up into the sky, they plummeted downward.

"Houston, we have a problem," Cornwall said with a whimper.

"Ladies and gentlemen, please restore your seats to the upright position!" said Devon.

Just then Sir Ruber and his servants appeared at the cliff. Somehow, they had managed to break free from the Ogre's lair.

Ruber ordered his minions to go after the dragon. He pushed the Griffin and the others off the cliff.

When Ayden saw the Griffin flying after them he quickly reversed his direction and faced the monstrous bird. The Griffin charged Ayden. Thinking quickly, Ayden came to an abrupt halt. This took the Griffin by surprise. Unable to stop his charge, the Griffin went flying into a pile of boulders at the top of the cliff.

Suddenly the boulders tumbled in an avalanche right on top of Sir Ruber.

In the meantime, Devon and Cornwall braced themselves. They were plummeting toward the ground at a terrific speed.

"Assume the crash position!" Cornwall warned Kayley and Garrett. "So long! Good-bye!"

"Help!" shrieked Devon. "Mayday! Mayday!"

And with that they tumbled to the ground and came to rest in a pond at the foot of the mountain.

Miraculously, they were unharmed.

"We did it!" exclaimed Kayley. "We did it! I can't believe it, we did it!"

"Congratulations," said Garrett.

Kayley took Garrett's hand and lovingly placed it with hers on the handle of Excalibur.

"So this is Excalibur!" she said.

"Hey, can I hold it?" asked Cornwall. Both he and Devon began tugging at the sword.

"No," said Garrett. "Excalibur only belongs in the hands of Arthur. C'mon, Kayley."

Garrett took Excalibur and led the others through the forest.

After they had walked for some time, Kayley asked, "Garrett, do you think my mother's safe?"

"If she's anything like you," replied Garrett, "I'm sure she's fine. Come. We must hurry. There isn't much time left."

They had only to walk a short distance further before Kayley noticed a patch of light up ahead.

"Garrett, up ahead," she pointed. "The sky!"

"The end of the Forbidden Forest," said Garrett.

Kayley grabbed Garrett by the hand and pulled him, eager to leave the Forbidden Forest. But Garrett would not move.

"It's okay," he said. "You go ahead."

Kayley bounded to the edge of the forest. Once there, she peered out beyond the last few trees. Standing on the horizon was a castle that seemed to sparkle in the sunlight. She knew instantly what the castle was.

"Camelot!" she exclaimed.

Soon, Garrett, Devon, and Cornwall joined her.

"The first two-headed dragon in Camelot!" said Cornwall, upon seeing the castle. "We'll be famous!"

"I can see us on the poster now," said Devon. "'Presenting the wonderful Devon and his little head, Cornwall.'"

"Why don't you shut up?" said Cornwall, insulted. "How 'bout 'Cornwall and his obnoxious talking wart'?"

"Knock it off!" said Garrett angrily.

"What's eating him?" asked Cornwall.

"Envy, poor lad," replied Devon. Then he told Garrett, "I'm sure there'll be a place in Camelot for you, Garrett. Maybe a job as a stable boy. It's a stable job."

But Garrett didn't laugh at the dragon's joke. In fact, he did not seem happy at all, despite the fact that he was now certain Arthur would have Excalibur again.

"Oh, Garrett," said Kayley. She was still overwhelmed by the sight of the castle. "It's so beautiful. I wish you could see it."

"I've seen it, remember?" replied Garrett sullenly. "And there was no place for me."

Kayley was surprised at Garrett's tone of voice. "Garrett, what's wrong?" she asked him.

"Take Excalibur to Arthur," said Garrett. "You don't have much time." Then he turned and started back into the forest.

"But, we'll deliver the sword *together*," said Kayley, catching up with him.

"No," said Garrett. "You deliver it. I don't belong in that world. C'mon, Ayden."

And with that Garrett and Ayden retreated further into the Forbidden Forest.

Kayley wasn't sure what to do. A part of her wanted to run after Garrett. She even thought she'd be willing to spend the rest of her life in the Forbidden Forest with him. That was how much she loved him.

But another part of her knew she had to go to Camelot. She had to return Excalibur to Arthur. And she had to save her mother.

She watched helplessly as Garrett disappeared into the forest. She made no move to chase after him. Instead, with Devon and Cornwall by her side, she turned around and left the forest.

She began her journey to Camelot.

"Forget about him," Cornwall told Kayley as they headed toward Camelot. "You're better off alone. He walks funny. He even looks funny. People throw darts at him."

Devon shot Cornwall an angry stare. "How can you be so cold-blooded?" he asked.

"It's easy," replied Cornwall. "I'm a reptile."

But Kayley wasn't listening to the bickering dragon. Instead she was lost in thought, confused by her emotions. As much as she knew it was her duty to go to

Camelot, she could not stop thinking of Garrett.

"I don't belong in that world . . ." she remembered Garrett saying.

Kayley tightened her grip around the handle of Excalibur. Engraved into the handle were the three rings that symbolized Camelot. They began to pulsate against her palm.

"I don't belong in that world." She heard Garrett's words again.

"But you belong in mine," she said quietly to herself. Then she turned to Devon and Cornwall and said, "I'm going back for him."

She spun around and headed back to the Forbidden Forest. But as soon as she had reached the first clump of trees that led into the dark forest, a hand reached from out of nowhere and yanked Excalibur away from her.

It was Sir Ruber. And beside him were Spike Slinger and Bowhands and his other minions.

"I'll take that!" said Ruber upon grabbing the sword. He held it high. "Excalibur — mine forever!"

Then Ruber pointed the sword at Kayley and waved it at her. "You know," he began, in a threatening tone of voice, "you've been very annoying — for a girl!"

12

Bittersweet Reunion

"I've waited ten years to hold this sword," Ruber said to Kayley. "And now I'll make it mine forever."

Spike Slinger grabbed Kayley and held her tightly. Then Ruber pulled the vial of magic potion out from under his cape and poured a droplet on his palm. His hand began to sizzle, filling the air with green smoke.

"Prepare for a dawning of a new age!" he said, shaking his hand at Kayley. "It's hot!"

Then Ruber placed Excalibur into his smoking hand. Suddenly, his arm began to spin — faster and faster and faster. Soon his hand, together with Excalibur, was nothing but a blur.

Slowly, Ruber's arms stopped spinning. Only now his arm and Excalibur had blended into one monstrous weapon.

"No!" shrieked Kayley as Ruber proudly raised his new swordarm into the air.

"Bring on the darkness!" Ruber laughed. "Bring on the gloom! We are the army of death and doom!"

At that, all of Ruber's minions cheered.

All except Bladebeak. Kayley could see that Bladebeak was starting to become just a little bit too frightened of Ruber.

"Don't worry, little girl," Ruber said to Kayley. "I'll see that Arthur gets this back — or *in* the back, as the case may be. Throw her in the wagon!"

Spike Slinger obeyed and threw Kayley into one of Ruber's waiting wagons.

Kayley tumbled into the wagon, head over heels. But when she looked up her heart leaped for joy. For also in the wagon was her mother. And she was safe and sound.

"Kayley!" exclaimed Juliana happily.

"Mother!" said Kayley, throwing herself into her mother's hug.

"Oh, thank heavens you're safe," said Juliana.

But Kayley was soon in tears. "I've failed you, Mother," she cried. "Now Camelot will be lost."

"No, dear," said Juliana. "You were brave."

Just then they looked up to see Ruber looking at them through the window.

"What a touching reunion," Ruber said with a laugh. "But let's get to work. I'll terrorize the people. Juliana, you betray the king. And remember, if you don't —"

A minion with a frightening hatchet for a foot pointed a spear at Kayley.

"If you don't," Ruber finished telling Juliana, "you'll never see your daughter alive again!"

Kayley could see that her mother had no choice but to help Ruber.

"Don't lose hope!" Juliana told Kayley.

And with that Spike Slinger pulled her mother from the back of the wagon and forced her to sit up front.

13

It Takes Two to Fly

Cornwall and Devon peeked out from the boulder they were hiding behind. They had seen everything and were lucky not to be caught themselves. Now they knew that Kayley was in great trouble. Thinking quickly, they returned to the Forbidden Forest and looked everywhere until they found Garrett, sitting by a pond.

"Damsel in distress!" they shouted frantically. "Damsel in distress!"

"I say, Garrett," said Devon. "Something awful's happened. Kayley's been captured."

"And Ruber's got Excalibur!" added Cornwall.

"What?" said Garrett, rising to his feet. "Take me to her! C'mon, Ayden!"

"They're halfway to Camelot by now," said Cornwall.

"We'd have to fly to get there in time," said Devon.

By now Cornwall and Devon were so angry at Sir Ruber — and so concerned about Kayley — that they didn't stop to remember they did not know how to fly. Instead, smoke and sparks began shooting out of their nostrils. Their wings began flapping wildly. It was as if a giant motor was revving up in their body. Before long they had lifted themselves up into the air and begun to fly.

"I detest that foul barbarian!" said Devon.

"I'm with you on that one," said Cornwall. "That foul barbarian!"

"Wait till we get our hands on him!" said Devon.

"We'll show him a thing or two!" added Cornwall.

"Hey," Garrett called to the dragon from the ground. "You're flying!"

Devon and Cornwall suddenly stopped in midair and looked down.

"Gosh, he's right!" said Devon. "We *are* flying!"

"I did it!" exclaimed Cornwall. "I'm great! I love me! I did it!"

"Excuse me, egomaniac," interrupted Devon. "You mean *I* did it!"

"No, you — !" Cornwall shot back.

By this time the two-headed dragon had become so angry with each other that they forgot to concentrate on flying. All at once their wings stopped fluttering. The smoke from their nostrils dwindled.

They began to fall.

SPLASH! The dragon fell into a pool of mud.

"Don't you get it?" asked Garrett, after the dragon popped its heads out of the pool of sludge. "The only reason you can't fly is because you can't agree on anything. There must be something you agree on. You both love Kayley, don't you?"

Cornwall and Devon smiled at each other. The very thought of Kayley was enough to make their wings flutter. Before long they found themselves flapping and twisting, twisting and turning, turning and sparking. Then, just as they had hoped, they managed to lift themselves out of the dirty mud and into the air once again.

"All aboard!" Devon said to Garrett.

"Yes, hand over your ticket and put your luggage in the overhead compartment," added Cornwall.

Garrett smiled. He happily climbed onto the dragon's back. Then, without further ado, Cornwall and Devon took off for Camelot.

14

Attack on Camelot

Thunder clouds were beginning to gather. The skies were growing dark. The Griffin was circling high above Camelot.

Kayley could see all this through the little window of her wagon.

They were nearing Camelot.

"Wagons approaching!" she heard the guard at the gate shout.

Slowly, the great drawbridge to Camelot lowered and the wagons moved across it.

Kayley could see Sir Ruber and her mother. Juliana was sitting in the front of the wagon. Sir Ruber was riding alongside.

"Not a word," she heard Ruber warn her mother.

Juliana turned and looked back at Kayley with a worried expression. Kayley wanted to shout out to her mother, but couldn't. Her hands were tied behind her back and a gag was tied around her mouth. Not only that, but Swordhands was holding a spear to her neck!

The wagon stopped as the guard of Camelot checked to identify the passengers. Once he saw that Lady Juliana, wife of Sir Lionel, was among them, he let the wagons through without any trouble.

As the wagons moved along Kayley could see they were heading straight for the castle where King Arthur lived. Along the way she could see all the people of Camelot as they went about their daily business. Some knights were patrolling the battlements, talking and laughing as they did so. Some merchants were conducting business, haggling over the price of a bag of rice or a small carpet. There were even some children playing hide-and-seek. Kayley wished she could warn the people of the danger.

Just then the wagon hit a bump in the road. Everyone inside was thrown off balance, even Swordhands. Thinking quickly, Kayley kicked Swordhands. Then she began looking around for something to cut her ropes with, but there was nothing.

Then a shadow fell over Kayley. She looked up. It was Bladebeak.

"Bladebeak, at your service," said the monstrous creature that had once been a rooster.

At that, Kayley cowered, fearing the worst. To her surprise, however, Bladebeak took his sharp beak and cut Kayley free.

Kayley wasted no time. She burst out of the wagon just as quickly as she could. "It's a trick!" she shouted to the Camelot guards. "It's a trick!"

"Attack!" Sir Ruber commanded his minions. "Seal off the castle!"

All of Sir Ruber's horrid minions leaped out of their wagons and rushed toward the castle. The guards in the courtyard instantly gave chase, but they were too late. The minions had blocked off the castle and were keeping the guards at bay.

Sir Ruber, at the head of his army, rode his horse up the steps of the castle, knocking down guards as he went. Spike Slinger pounded his mighty arms on the huge wooden door of the castle until it gave way. There were some guards inside the castle, but Spike Slinger and the others easily knocked them down.

Now the path was cleared and Ruber took advantage. He galloped into the castle and headed for the room of the Round Table. It was there he knew he would find Arthur. It was there he knew he would destroy the king and claim the throne of Camelot as his own.

15

Dragons to the Rescue

"I must help the king!" exclaimed Kayley upon seeing Ruber break into the castle. "Are you going to be all right, Mother?"

"Yes, dear," said Juliana. "Go!"

"Don't worry," said Bladebeak as he stood beside Juliana and his wife, Henrietta the hen. "She'll be fine."

Seeing that her mother would be safe, Kayley hurried toward the battlements.

She weaved in and around the battling guards and minions until she reached a scaffolding that climbed the side of the castle itself.

Some distance up the side of the castle was a window. Knowing she could enter the castle through the window without being seen, Kayley quickly began climbing the scaffolding. But no sooner had she started off in the direction of the window than the Griffin appeared in the sky and swooped down upon her, shattering the scaffolding as he did so.

Kayley tried to run, but stopped when she saw she was surrounded by a group of Sir Ruber's minions. With the Griffin coming from one direction and the minions coming from the other, Kayley thought that all was surely lost.

Suddenly she heard a familiar voice from above. "Fasten your seat belts and push up your dining trays," said the voice. "We're coming in for an emergency landing!"

Kayley looked up. Diving down from the

sky were Devon and Cornwall. And the dragon wasn't alone. On its back was Garrett!

"Garrett!" shouted Kayley happily.

"Sorry I'm late," Garrett said as he leaped off Devon and Cornwall and began bashing the minions. "Traffic was murder!"

Garrett pulled Kayley to a safe place. It was there they shared a warm embrace.

Afterward, Kayley noticed Devon and Cornwall hovering in the air.

"You're flying!" Kayley said to her two-headed friend.

"Yes," said the dragon. "We're frequent flyers now!"

"Where's Ruber?" Garrett asked Kayley.

"He has the king trapped inside the castle," said Kayley. "But there's no way in."

"There's one way in," remembered Garrett. "The stables."

Garrett took Kayley by the hand to lead her across the battle-filled courtyard to the stables. But before they could get started, the Griffin appeared, ready to attack.

Sensing the Griffin's presence, Garrett jumped in front of Kayley and began swiping at the huge bird with his staff. But the Griffin was too powerful and Garrett began to feel his strength go.

Just then Garrett and Kayley heard a loud shriek from above. It was Ayden. With his silver wings spread wide, Ayden swooped down and charged the Griffin, striking him squarely between the eyes.

"Finally, silver wings, you're mine!" the Griffin said to Ayden. Then he charged the falcon.

But just then Devon and Cornwall swooped down between the two birds.

"Excuse me," Devon said to the Griffin.

"Pick on somebody your own size," added Cornwall.

The Griffin lunged at the dragon. The dragon opened both its mouths and shot a hot blast of fire at the Griffin, scorching him all over until he was unable to attack.

Garrett and Kayley again headed toward the stables, but Ruber's minions chased them. Kayley grabbed Garrett's hand and together they jumped into a horse-drawn wagon filled with hay. Garrett pulled on the reins. The horses reared up and pulled the wagon across the courtyard.

"Hang on!" Garrett told Kayley.

"What are you doing?" asked Kayley as she grabbed the side of the wagon bench.

"Driving!"

"Left!" shouted Kayley, giving Garrett directions.

CRASH! They knocked over a vegetable stand.

"Excuse me!" Garrett shouted to the people in the courtyard. "Coming through!"

CRASH! They knocked into a group of guards.

"Sorry . . ." Garrett shouted at the stunned guards. "Pardon us!"

"Next time, maybe I should drive," suggested Kayley.

Finally, they crashed into the stables, and landed on soft sacks of grain.

Garrett knew where he was now. He quickly felt around the floor of the stable until he found what he was looking for: a trapdoor. He opened the door and lowered himself and Kayley into the ground. Once underground, Kayley saw that they were in a dark tunnel.

"These tunnels lead to the Round Table room," Garrett told Kayley.

They had to crouch in order to make their way along the tunnels. Although it was too dark for Kayley to see, Garrett seemed to know the way.

"I can't see," said Kayley.

"Don't worry," said Garrett. "This time I'll be *your* eyes."

And he was. Using his staff as a guide, Garrett quickly moved through the tunnels.

They were on their way to the Round Table. Kayley only hoped they would make it there in time!

16

The Stone
and the Sword

Suddenly Kayley heard a voice up ahead.

"So many memories in this room," the voice said. "It makes me sick!"

It was Sir Ruber! His voice was coming from the Round Table room. She knew at once that he was talking to King Arthur.

"You said everyone at this table was equal," she heard Sir Ruber continue, in a threatening tone of voice. "Well, I have something sweeter — *revenge!*"

Next Kayley heard a loud *CLANG!* Was it the sound of swords hitting? King Arthur was in danger.

"We've got to hurry!" Kayley told Garrett.

Again Kayley heard the sound of swords fighting. She and Garrett hurried through the maze of tunnels until the sound got louder and louder. Soon Kayley saw a dim light up ahead. It was coming from a small grate.

"Here it is," said Garrett. "Through this grate is the Round Table."

Kayley could just see through the holes in the grate. What she had feared was true. King Arthur and Sir Ruber were locked in combat. Ruber had Arthur pinned to the Round Table itself. King Arthur was protecting himself with a spear, but Sir Ruber clearly had the upper hand. In fact, his hand was still completely fused with Excalibur.

Kayley gasped as Sir Ruber brought the sword down, but Arthur rolled out of the way. Excalibur smashed into the Round Table.

"I'm going to have more fun getting rid of you than when I got rid of Sir Lionel," Kayley heard Ruber tell Arthur.

Upon hearing this Kayley became more angry than ever before. *So it was Sir Ruber who killed Father,* she now knew.

Together she and Garrett pushed at the grate and rose up through the floor of the Round Table chamber.

Kayley knew she had to do something to save the king. Thinking quickly, she ran to the other side of the room where some repairs had been left unfinished. There was some scaffolding. And, most importantly, there was a piece of timber tied to a long rope.

"I may not survive, but you'll never destroy the ideals of Camelot," Kayley heard King Arthur tell Ruber as she climbed the scaffolding.

"Well, I've got to start somewhere," laughed Ruber. "Say hello to your new king!"

"You're no king!" Arthur shot back, darting away from Ruber's deadly blows.

"You're right," agreed Ruber. "Perhaps I'm more of a god!"

Ruber kicked King Arthur. King Arthur fell back against what was left of the Round Table. He was groggy and barely able to defend himself. Upon seeing this, Sir Ruber raised Excalibur and prepared to bring it down for the final blow.

"I will not serve a false king!" shouted Kayley from behind Ruber.

Ruber turned. "You!" he shouted with surprise.

Kayley had climbed onto the slab of timber that was hanging from the scaffolding. She had leaped off the scaffolding and was now swinging through the air, riding the timber like a surfboard. She was headed straight for Sir Ruber. Ruber raised Excalibur for protection, but it was too late. Kayley smashed into him. Together they went careening through the window and down to the landing below.

When Kayley rose to her feet she noticed that they had landed right next to the ring of stones. She knew at once that the one in the center was the magical stone her father had once told her about. The true home of Excalibur.

Just then Ruber popped up from behind her.

"You're in the way," Ruber said, moving around the stones toward Kayley. "Just like your father."

Kayley stumbled backward. Ruber raised Excalibur.

"Since you're dying to be like him," he began, "let's see if I can't help you out."

And with that Ruber brought the sword down, just missing her by a hair. He raised the sword again.

Then Ruber received a blow from behind. It was Garrett, coming to Kayley's rescue. He smashed his staff against

Ruber's back. But Ruber swiveled around and knocked Garrett to the ground. Then he broke Garrett's staff in two.

"You probably needed that," Ruber mocked, pointing to the broken staff. "Here, I'll make sure you don't trip."

He grabbed Garrett by the hair and yanked him to his feet.

"Oops, I lied." Ruber laughed. Then he tossed Garrett toward Kayley.

Kayley and Garrett suddenly found themselves backed up against the center stone. Before them stood Ruber. Like a wolf coming in for the kill he raised Excalibur into the air.

"Hold your ground until the last possible moment," Kayley whispered to Garrett.

The words instantly reminded Garrett of the lesson in survival he had taught Kayley when they were in the Forbidden Forest.

"And you give me the signal," Garrett whispered back.

"Two for the price of one," laughed Ruber,

Excalibur ready to plunge. "This must be my lucky day."

Ruber began to lower his deadly arm.

"Now!" Kayley whispered the signal to Garrett.

Kayley and Garrett leaped out of the way. Ruber's arm continued down, plunging Excalibur right into the center of the stone.

Ruber tried to pull the sword out, but it — and his arm — wouldn't budge. Suddenly a surge of electricity seemed to crisscross over the stone. The current creeped up the sword and through Ruber's arm.

"NOOO!" Ruber screamed.

Then there was a loud clap of thunder and a bright flash. A burst of colored lights, bright reds, greens, and yellows, completely engulfed Ruber.

An instant later he was gone. Nothing was left but a wisp of dark smoke.

Nothing was left but Excalibur.

Suddenly, the magical light that had destroyed Ruber had spread to the rest of Camelot. Then, as if a terrible curse were being lifted, one by one Ruber's minions began to change back to their human bodies.

Gone was Spike Slinger. Gone was Bowhands. And Bladebeak had changed back to his old self, the rooster.

Even Devon and Cornwall were changed. The magic light had split them apart. One look at each other and they panicked. They jumped back together, happy to remain in one body with two heads.

Soon the magic light retreated back to the magic stone of three rings. With Ruber gone, all that remained was Excalibur, safely lodged in the glowing stone.

A hand reached down and pulled Excalibur out of the stone. It was the only hand that could have done so, the hand of King Arthur.

Everyone in Camelot cheered.

The king had been saved.

17

The Newest Knights of the Round Table

That afternoon a great festival was held in Camelot. Bells chimed. Flowers were strung across the walls of the castle. Ribbons were hanging from the ceiling.

The sun was shining brightly through the stained glass windows of the Round Table chamber. The chamber was crowded with people, all happy that peace had once again come to Camelot.

Kayley and Juliana were there. So were Devon, Cornwall, and Ayden. The Knights of the Round Table all had taken their seats.

At the front of the room stood Garrett. Before him was King Arthur, Excalibur raised proudly in his hand.

Kayley stepped forward.

"Kayley," said Juliana. "You forgot this."

Juliana gave Kayley the shield that had once belonged to Sir Lionel. Then Kayley took her place beside Garrett. They kneeled.

"I dub thee Sir Garrett," Arthur announced as he touched Garrett's shoulders with Excalibur. "And I dub thee Lady Kayley," he announced doing the same to Kayley. "Rise."

Kayley and Garrett stood up. They were beaming with pride.

"You have reminded us that a kingdom's strength is not based on the strength of the king, but the strength of the people," said Arthur. "From this day forward, you will both sit as Knights of the Round Table."

Everyone in the room cheered.

"Is this everything you ever wanted?" Kayley asked Garrett.

"Not quite everything," replied Garrett.

He leaned over to give Kayley a loving kiss. In time Kayley and Garrett were married. Devon and Cornwall became their trusted partners, and Ayden, their best friend. They courageously served King Arthur and the people of Camelot.

And like all good heroes, they lived happily ever after.